I'm Reading About

UTAH

The Beehive State!

GALLOPADE

by Carole Marsh

Printed and Manufactured in Peachtree City, GA., USA
www.gallopade.com

Book design: John Hanson

Editorial manager: Janice Baker

Utah is a great state.
It is one of a kind.

What makes Utah special?
Let's read about it
and see!

Who lived in Utah first?

Native Americans did!

They moved around to find food.
They hunted for animals to eat.
They fished in Utah's rivers.
They gathered fruits and seeds and nuts.

EXPLORERS

Some of the first explorers came to Utah in 1776.
They were Spanish priests from New Mexico.
Their names were Father Dominguez
and Father Escalante.

They wrote about the area in their journals.
They also made maps.

SETTLEMENT

A group of Mormons traveled west across the United States.
They started the first settlements in Utah.
One of them was Salt Lake City.

Mormons moved to Utah to find religious freedom.

Salt Lake City

STATEHOOD

Utah was the 45th state
to join the United States of America!

Isn't it great,
to be a state!
I bet Utah
could hardly wait!

Utah became a state in 1896.

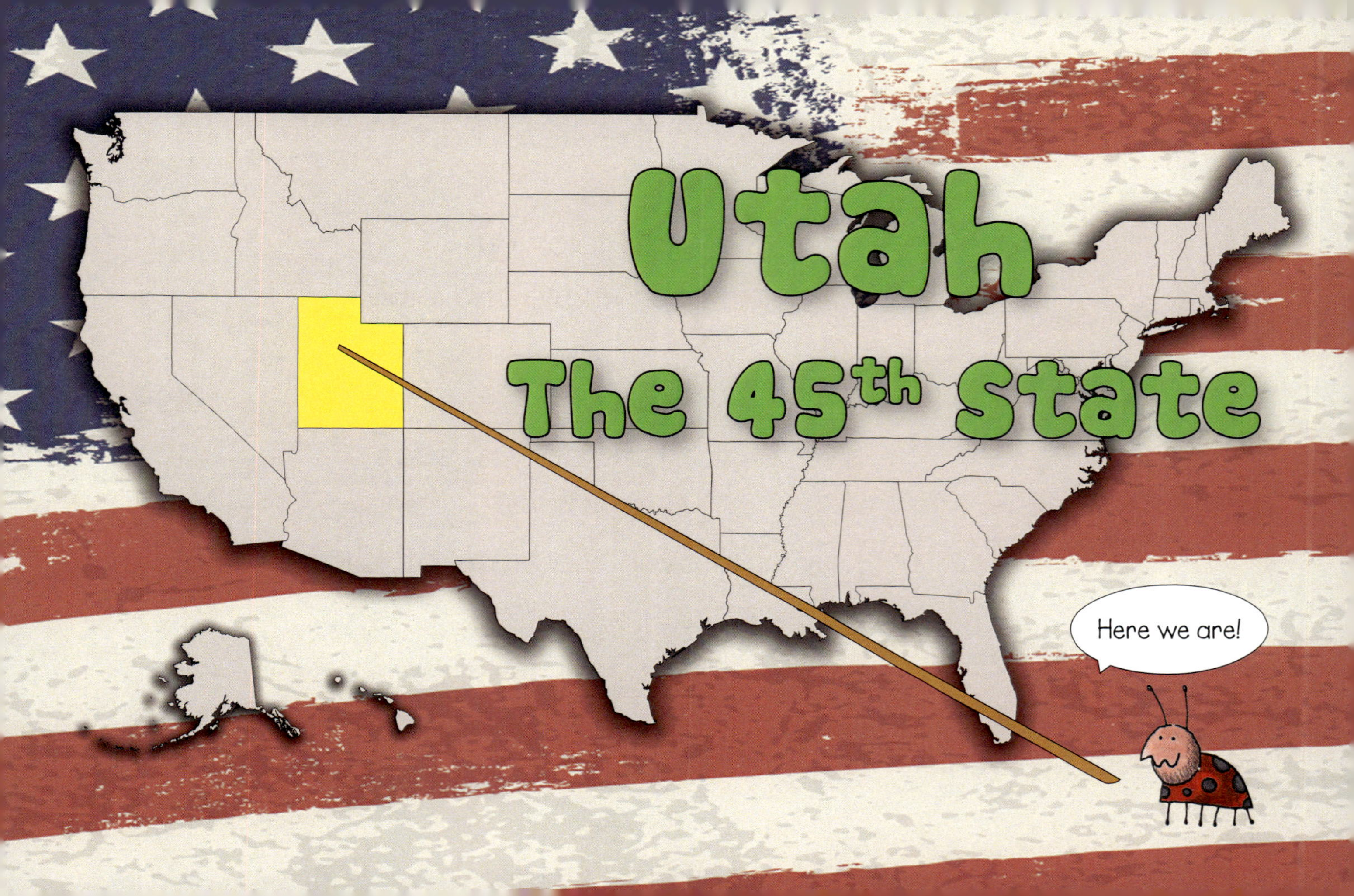
Utah
The 45th State
Here we are!

FLAG

I am the state flag.

What color am I?
I am red, white, and blue.

Look at me.
What else do you see?

I fly high over the state of Utah!

CAPITAL

Say hello to Salt Lake City,
the capital city of Utah!

There is an important building in Salt Lake City.
It is the State Capitol.
Utah's laws are made there!

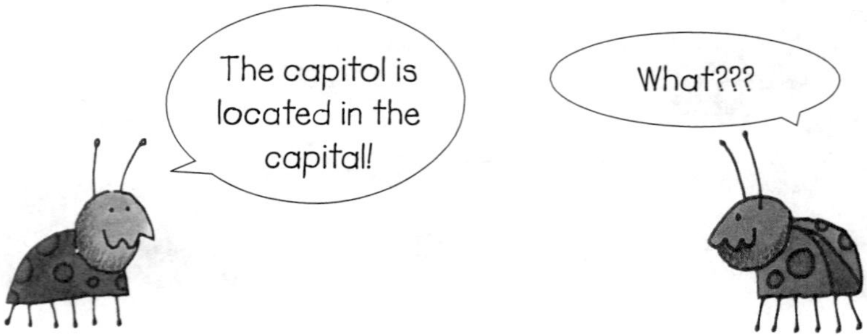

Capitol

SEAL

I am a seal,
but I am not the State Seal.
If I were, I would be very important.
I would be stamped on many official papers.
(Ouch, that might hurt!)

THE GREAT SEAL OF THE STATE OF UTAH
INDUSTRY
1847
1896
Now, that's official!

NICKNAME

State nicknames are fun!
State nicknames are great!
They share fun facts
about each state!

Utah's nickname is "The Beehive State."

Utah pioneers used the beehive as their emblem. It symbolized working together like bees do!

The Beehive State

BORDERS

Look at Utah.
Utah is in a region called "the West."

Utah borders five other states.
Find them on the map!

Borders

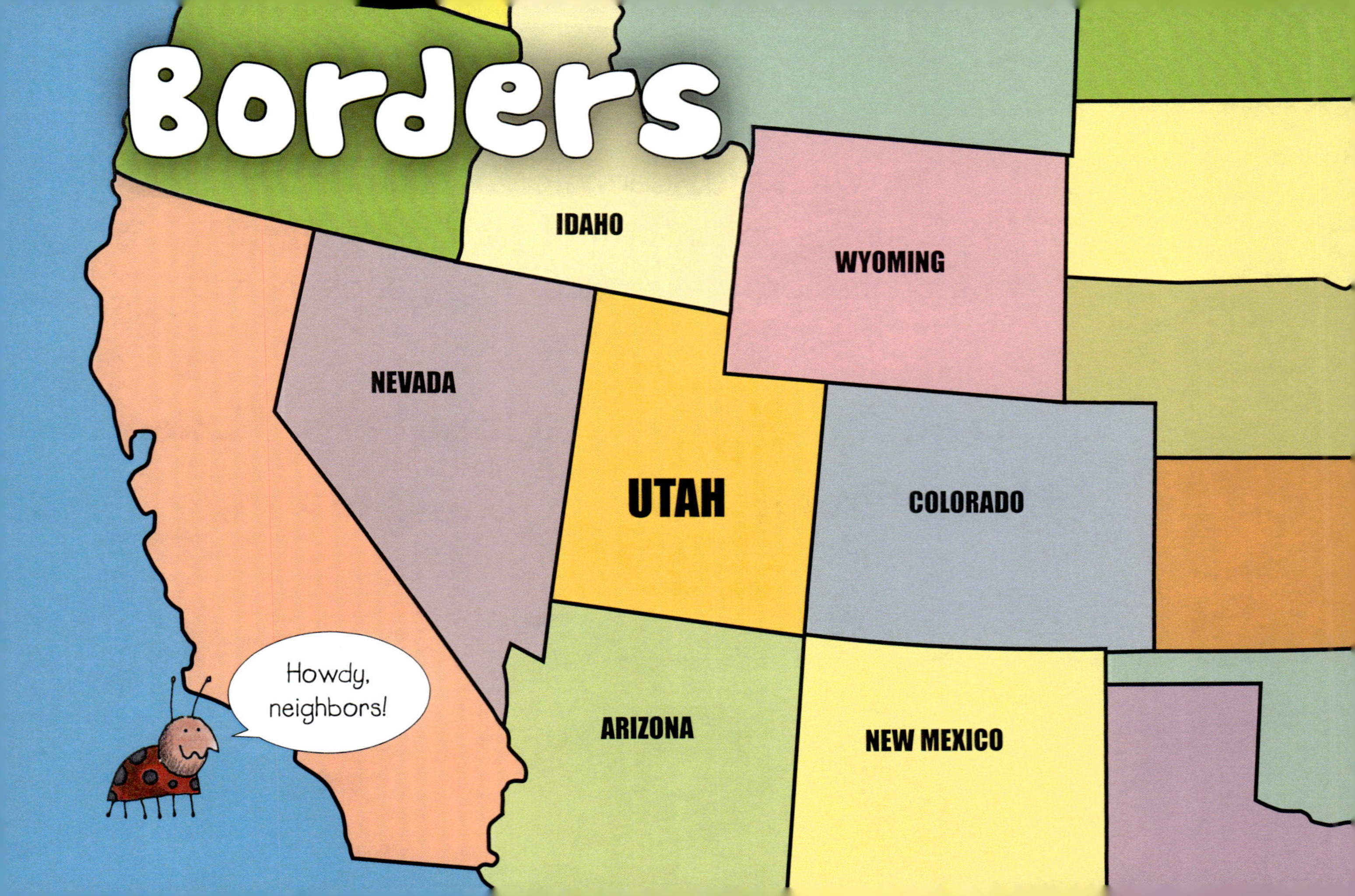
IDAHO
WYOMING
NEVADA
UTAH
COLORADO
ARIZONA
NEW MEXICO
Howdy, neighbors!

COUNTIES

Utah is divided into 29 counties.
Counties are a form of local government.
Counties provide services that people need!
Those services include:

Schools **Parks** **Libraries** **Police**
Firefighters **and More!**

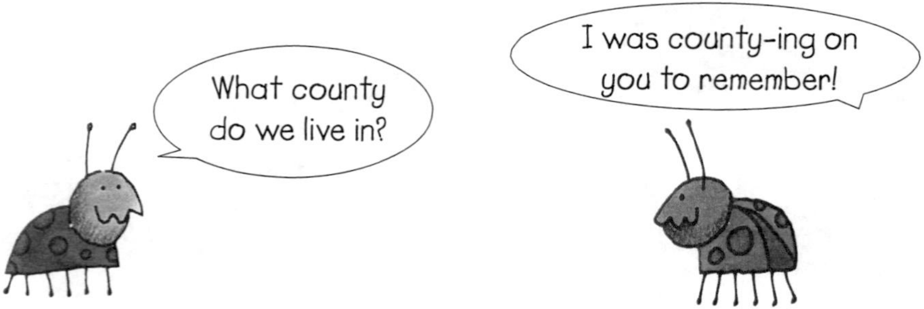

Counties

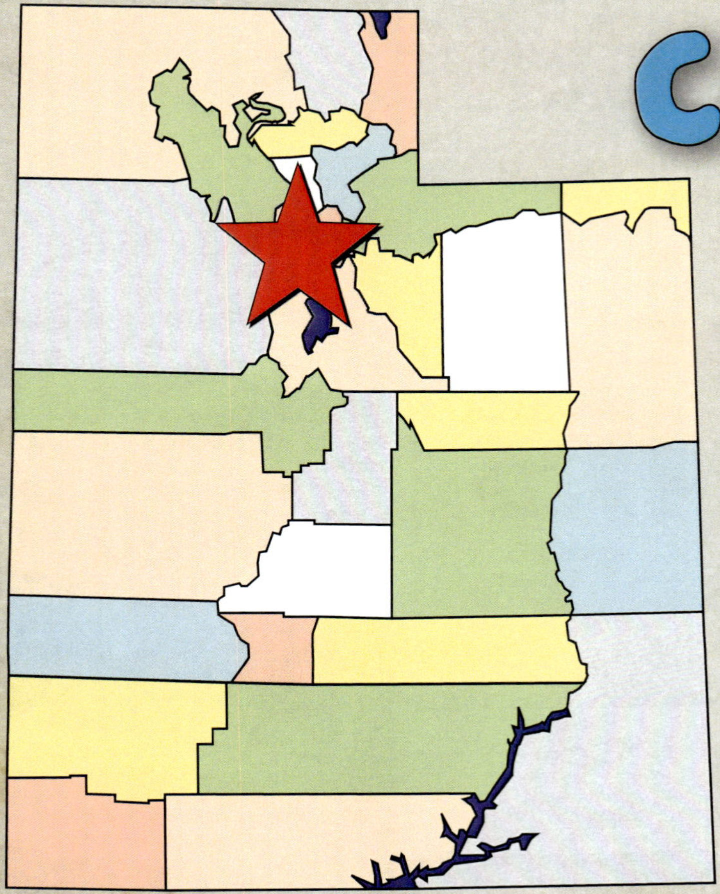

Many famous people

Brigham Young
Founder of Salt Lake City

John Browning
Gun inventor known as the "Father of Modern Firearms"

J. Willard Marriott
Founder of the Marriott hotel chain

call our state home!

PEOPLE

Philo Farnsworth

Invented technology that led to modern television

Olene S. Walker

First female governor of Utah

Donny and Marie Osmond

Singers and television personalities

California Seagull

BIRD

I am the state bird, and I fly
over Utah, proud and high.

As I fly, up in the sky,
I flap my wings to tell you "Hi!"

The Utah state bird is the California Seagull.

Sego Lily

I am the Sego Lily.
I am the state flower.

I grow where it's warm and sunny.
I bloom in spring and summer.
I help make Utah beautiful!

Look at me! Smell me!
My blossoms look like beautiful white goblets!

FLOWER

Quaking Aspen

I am a Quaking Aspen—I'm the state tree.
All over Utah is where to find me.

My roots run deep, they keep me strong.
I can live for a hundred years—that's very long!

I stand up straight, big and tall.
Don't climb too high—it would hurt to fall!

TREE

Honeybee

I am the Honeybee.
I am the state insect.

I might sting you if you bother me.
But really, I am your friend.

I carry pollen from flower to flower.
I make honey.
I help Utah crops grow.

BZZZZZZZZZZZZ!

INSECT

Rivers

Let's go to the river!

We can wade in the water.
We can fish in the sun.

We can float on an inner tube
There's no end to the fun!

Utah's rivers are home to many animals:

Birds **Deer** **Snakes** **Frogs** **Fish** **and More!**

RIVERS

Rocky Mountains

MOUNTAINS

Utah's Rocky Mountains are the place to be.
Hiking, fishing, camping—
fun for you and me.

Winter weather brings lots of snow.
Temperatures drop to freezing and below!

Salt Flats

SALT FLATS

Utah's Bonneville Salt Flats is a unique land feature. It is very flat land covered with a layer of white salt. It looks like a huge frozen lake!

The salt crust is almost 5 feet thick in the center of the Salt Flats.

Cars, trucks, and motorcycles race on the Salt Flats. Many land speed records have been set there!

The Great Salt Lake

The Great Salt Lake is in northern Utah.
After the Great Lakes, it is the largest lake in the U.S.

The Great Salt Lake is much saltier than seawater.
Fish cannot live in the salty water.

The brine shrimp is one of the only animals that can live in the Great Salt Lake.
It likes the salty water!

Utah Crops

Utah has many farms.
Why?
Because Utah has good soil and a mild climate!

Some of the top crops grown in Utah are:

Hay **Wheat** **Corn** **Cherries**

Sports in Utah

SPORTS

Baseball! Basketball! Football!
Utah has it all.

Whether you like to watch or play,
You are sure to have a ball!

Jazz **Starzz** **Cougars**

Utes

Aggies

& More!

Utah: Home of Promontory Summit
Choooo!
Choooo!
All Aboooooard!
UTAH
1896
CROSSROADS OF THE WEST
2007
E PLURIBUS UNUM

The first Transcontinental Railroad was completed in Promontory, Utah, in 1869!
The Transcontinental Railroad connected America's east and west coasts.
The railroad united America!

A huge celebration was held at Promontory Summit.

A golden spike was hammered into the rails!

GLOSSARY

beehive: place where bees live and make honey

climate: weather conditions in an area over a long period of time

emblem: an object that serves as a symbol

goblet: a bowl–shaped drinking cup

laws: rules made by the government

pollen: a yellow powder that helps plants make new plants

quaking: shaking or trembling

region: an area that has similar characteristics

settlement: the first community in an area

unique: something that is the only one of its kind